ALL ABOUT WOMEN'S COLLEGE GYMNASTICS

BY HEATHER RULE

SportsZone
An Imprint of Abdo Publishing
abdobooks.com

abdobooks.com

Published by Abdo Publishing, a division of ABDO, PO Box 398166, Minneapolis, Minnesota 55439. Copyright © 2021 by Abdo Consulting Group, Inc. International copyrights reserved in all countries. No part of this book may be reproduced in any form without written permission from the publisher. SportsZone™ is a trademark and logo of Abdo Publishing.

Printed in the United States of America, North Mankato, Minnesota
042020
092020

THIS BOOK CONTAINS RECYCLED MATERIALS

Cover Photo: Ben Liebenberg/AP Images
Interior Photos: Kyusung Gong/Icon Sportswire/AP Images, 4–5, 11; Charles Krupa/AP Images, 8; Katharine Lotze/Getty Images Sport/Getty Images, 13, 25; Brent Clark/Zuma Wire/Cal Sport Media/AP Images, 15; Aspen Photo/Shutterstock Images, 16; Kyle Okita/Cal Sport Media/Newscom, 17; Amy Sanderson/Zuma Wire/Cal Sport Media/AP Images, 19, 22; Jon Endow/Image of Sport/AP Images, 21; Sue Ogrocki/AP Images, 28; Rick Bowmer/AP Images, 29

Editor: Charly Haley
Series Designer: Megan Ellis

Library of Congress Control Number: 2019954392

Publisher's Cataloging-in-Publication Data

Names: Rule, Heather, author.
Title: All about women's college gymnastics / by Heather Rule
Description: Minneapolis, Minnesota : Abdo Publishing, 2021 | Series: Gymnastics zone | Includes online resources and index.
Identifiers: ISBN 9781532192333 (lib. bdg.) | ISBN 9781098210236 (ebook)
Subjects: LCSH: Gymnastics--Juvenile literature. | Universities and colleges--Sports--Juvenile literature. | Sports--History--Juvenile literature. | Gymnastics for children--Juvenile literature.
Classification: DDC 796.44--dc23

CONTENTS

CHAPTER 1
FINDING JOY IN GYMNASTICS 4

CHAPTER 2
HOW COLLEGE GYMNASTICS WORKS 12

CHAPTER 3
GETTING A PERFECT 10 18

CHAPTER 4
BACK TO SCHOOL 24

GLOSSARY 30
MORE INFORMATION 31
ONLINE RESOURCES 31
INDEX.. 32
ABOUT THE AUTHOR 32

CHAPTER 1

FINDING JOY IN GYMNASTICS

The crowd cheered when the music started. Gymnast Katelyn Ohashi moved from her frozen spot standing on the floor in her sparkling blue leotard. She shook her arms and hips in motion with the music. She lifted her head to show a smiling face and bobbing brown curls. From there she ran across the mat for her first tumbling pass, sticking the landing with both feet firmly in place.

Katelyn Ohashi's 2019 floor routine was fun and energetic.

She kept a smile on her face as she continued her routine for the next 90 seconds. Anyone could see how much fun she was having. She showed off confident looks during her dance moves. Her University of California, Los Angeles (UCLA) teammates looked on from the sidelines with anticipation and excitement. They even mimicked some of her moves and motions in between their cheers.

VIRAL MOMENT WINS ESPY

For her viral, perfect 10 floor exercise at the Collegiate Classic, Ohashi took home two awards at the 2019 ESPYs, an annual awards show by the sports TV network ESPN. She won the Best Viral Moment and Best Play awards. She was the third female athlete to ever win in the Best Play category. Just six months after her performance, a video of the routine had been viewed more than 125 million times online.

Ohashi ended with one final turn. Then she ran over toward the sidelines to high-five her line of thrilled teammates. A few gymnasts jumped up and down with their arms raised. They showed all 10 fingers on their hands, predicting Ohashi's score for the routine.

The judges at the Collegiate Classic meet in January 2019 agreed: Ohashi earned a perfect 10 for her floor exercise.

The fourth perfect 10 of Ohashi's career on the floor exercise helped give her team a total score of 49.700 in that event. It was the fifth-highest mark that a UCLA team had ever received. UCLA won the competition with a 197.700 score.

Ohashi had been through many challenges before she performed that fun routine. Ohashi started practicing gymnastics when she was three years old. She became an elite gymnast by age 12 with the goal of making the Olympics.

Before deciding to focus on college, Ohashi competed at the elite level and hoped to qualify for the Olympics.

But the more she trained and practiced, the less joy she had for the sport.

She struggled with injuries, too. She had a sore back right before her first senior competition at age 16. The injury kept getting worse. But Ohashi won the 2013 American Cup anyway. Then the next year, she injured her shoulder and needed surgery. These injuries kept her from competing for two years. She wasn't upset by this news. She was feeling so pressured by gymnastics that being told to stay away felt like a weight was lifted off her shoulders.

But during her time off, Ohashi found that she missed gymnastics. After many doctor appointments, she was cleared to start training again. Though she could once again do gymnastics, her body couldn't take the impact of elite competition. That's when she switched her path to college gymnastics at UCLA.

Ohashi never made it to the Olympics, like she had hoped. But she didn't mind. Instead, she retired from elite gymnastics in 2015 and switched to college gymnastics, where she could compete more and train less. This helped her find her passion for gymnastics again. College allowed Ohashi to make gymnastics a part of her life instead of all of it.

Ohashi had fun with the sport in college. She did well, too. She graduated in 2019, finishing her career with 11 perfect 10s (nine in floor exercise and two on the balance beam). Ohashi helped her 2018 UCLA team win a national championship. She was a champion nationally and in her conference on floor exercise as a junior.

Perhaps the best thing about her gymnastics journey was that Ohashi found joy competing as a collegiate athlete. Elite gymnastics can be all about getting to the podium—focusing exclusively on winning medals. At UCLA Ohashi trained to have fun, grow her skills, and feel good about her work. College gymnastics helped Ohashi rediscover her love for the sport.

Ohashi celebrates with the UCLA student section during a meet against Arizona State.

CHAPTER 2

HOW COLLEGE GYMNASTICS WORKS

College gymnastics focuses a lot on competition. The National Collegiate Athletic Association (NCAA) limits gymnastics teams to 20 hours of training each week. By contrast the USA Elite Program gives gymnasts a chance to train and compete for a spot on the national team, which competes in the Olympics. Elite gymnasts might spend up to 40 hours a week in the gym.

Valorie Kondos Field led UCLA to seven NCAA titles as head coach from 1991 to 2019.

Gymnasts who compete in college have time to get an education along the way. The NCAA women's gymnastics season runs from January to April with about 15 meets. A typical head-to-head meet between two teams includes four events in women's gymnastics: vault, uneven parallel bars, balance beam, and floor exercise. Six gymnasts compete on each event with two tries each. A gymnast's score is the average from her two tries. Then the team takes the top five scores for each event.

JOIN THE CLUB

College athletes can also compete in gymnastics clubs. The National Association of Intercollegiate Gymnastics Clubs hosted its first national championships in 1989 and has 143 clubs in 38 states. The association supports male and female club gymnasts with the goal of promoting gymnastics "for the love of the sport."

Alexis Hankins of the Ohio State Buckeyes competes on floor exercise.

At the end of the season, the top 36 teams compete in regional competitions. Those have three rounds in early April. Eight teams, four all-around gymnasts, and 16 gymnasts who specialize in a certain event advance to the national championships.

At nationals, teams compete in the semifinal round, with the top two teams moving on to the finals. A team wins with the highest team score of five scores that count for each event. All-around and individual championships are given to the individual gymnasts who have the highest cumulative scores during the competition session on the first day.

In 2019, 82 schools had NCAA women's gymnastics programs with a total of approximately 3,500 gymnasts across the country. Sixty-one of the programs were in Division I, the highest level of NCAA competition. Six Division II schools have gymnastics programs, and 14 Division III schools offer women's gymnastics.

Amanda Bowman competes on vault for West Virginia University, a Division I school.

The Oklahoma Sooners women's gymnastics team celebrates its victory at the 2019 NCAA Championships.

All 82 gymnastics programs are eligible to compete in the NCAA Championships. Programs typically compete within their divisions throughout the year, but they are allowed to face different divisions.

The National Collegiate Gymnastics Association holds its own national competition at the end of each season to find the best in Division III gymnastics.

CHAPTER 3

GETTING A PERFECT 10

The University of Oklahoma's Brenna Dowell, a senior, stuck the landing at the end of a vault routine in March 2019. This helped her team pull ahead early, and the Sooners went on to win the meet against Alabama. Dowell's score was a perfect 10—her first of that season and the third of her college career.

The NCAA uses a perfect 10 scoring system. It's different from the Olympics. A gymnast starts an event with a score as high as 10.

Oklahoma's Brenna Dowell cheers after finishing a vault routine.

Then the judges take points off if the gymnast makes mistakes or doesn't do certain things. Finishing a routine with a perfect 10 score is rare.

Judges can deduct points based on how gymnasts perform certain parts of their routines. For example, NCAA gymnasts must stick their landings with both feet. A step or a hop on the landing will cost a gymnast a chance at a perfect 10. In the floor exercise, gymnasts must stick the landings or end in a controlled lunge. A wobble to check balance on the beam will get a deduction, too.

Six gymnasts from a team compete on each event during NCAA competitions. The top five scores are counted for the team total. The highest possible team score for four events is 200 points. Division I teams usually post team scores in the range of 197 to 198 points.

College gymnasts are very focused on teamwork. An Olympic gold medal is usually

Lynnzee Brown of the University of Denver celebrates with her teammates after finishing a floor routine.

the goal of an elite gymnast. An NCAA team championship is the biggest prize in college gymnastics. College gymnastics teams train together nearly every day for four years. They compete and work together for the team scores. Many college gymnasts love their sport's fun and inviting atmosphere. Teammates support each other. Elite gymnasts may compete against

their own teammates for gold medals. But when a college gymnast gets a perfect 10, her teammates will often jump around her and cheer excitedly. The teammates appear as happy as if they scored the perfect 10 themselves.

College gymnasts can perform more relaxed than elite gymnasts can. College gymnasts

College gymnastics is known for letting athletes show their personalities in their routines.

slap smiles on their faces as they bounce around to the music of their floor routines. Elite gymnasts concentrate on their individual routines which are more restrained and precise.

Elite gymnasts receive scores based on the difficulty level of their routines. But college gymnasts don't have to worry so much about doing the most difficult skills in order to get a high score. They're focused on performing their routines the best they can without mistakes.

Without worrying about really difficult moves, collegiate gymnasts are free to do fun dance moves in their competitions, such as moonwalking. Fans won't see these things in the Olympics. Those gymnasts need to perform tough elements like full-twisting switch leaps so they can get more points.

CHAPTER 4
BACK TO SCHOOL

It was March 16, 2019, the final home gymnastics meet for UCLA that year. Gymnast Kyla Ross made sure UCLA had a memorable victory over Utah State University. Ross finished her tumbling passes with no problems. She danced around, moving her heels up and down rhythmically with the music. One of the broadcasters said she had "never seen [Ross] smile with that pure-joy smile she's showing right now." The judges revealed the perfect 10. Then Ross—nicknamed "Kyla Boss"—was mobbed by

UCLA's Kyla Ross performs on the balance beam to earn a perfect 10.

her cheering UCLA teammates, creating a sea of blue, sparkling leotards.

That 10 score on the floor exercise gave Ross a "gym slam," or a perfect 10 on each of the four rotations. Ross had won Olympic gold with Team USA in 2012 in London, England. She retired from elite gymnastics in 2016 so she could be a student athlete in college.

In 2017 Ross and her UCLA teammate Madison Kocian became the first US Olympic

MEN'S COLLEGE GYMNASTICS

Men's college gymnastics started in 1938. The competition is a little different from the women's with the floor exercise, pommel horse, parallel bars, horizontal bar, rings, and vault events. Fifteen NCAA schools had men's gymnastics programs for the 2020 season. There were also eight schools in the Gymnastics Association of College Teams.

gold medalists to compete in NCAA gymnastics. Kocian won Olympic team gold and also silver on the uneven bars with Team USA in 2016 in Rio de Janeiro, Brazil. Kocian was the only member of that team who competed in college gymnastics after the Olympics.

Kocian and Ross won the 2018 NCAA team championship with UCLA by 0.0375 points. They beat the University of Oklahoma and Maggie Nichols. Nichols was an elite gymnast who won gold as part of the US team at the 2015 World Championships.

Nichols, known as "Swaggy Maggie" during her elite career, was the sixth gymnast in NCAA history to win all-around national titles in back-to-back seasons in 2018 and 2019.

Nichols finished her balance beam routine at the national championships in 2019 by landing evenly on the mat. She pumped both arms in

Maggie Nichols competes on the balance beam as part of the Perfect 10 Challenge in Oklahoma City in 2019.

celebration of her 9.9625 score. Like Ross, Nichols has two gym slams.

Other gymnasts have also switched from elite gymnastics to the NCAA. Courtney Kupets Carter competed with Team USA in the 2004 Olympics in Athens, Greece, winning a silver medal and a bronze medal on the uneven bars. Then she was a gymnast at the University of Georgia from 2006 to 2009. She finished college with four national team championships and nine individual NCAA titles. She was also a 15-time All-American. The Women's Collegiate Gymnastics Association awards All-American honors to the top 16 ranked gymnasts on each event and the all-around competition each season.

In 2017 Kupets Carter returned to Georgia to take over as its head coach. She had stood on the Olympic podium before winning NCAA titles. Now it was her turn to help the next generation of college gymnasts pursue their goal of winning an NCAA championship.

After the 2004 Olympics, Courtney Kupets Carter attended the University of Georgia and continued to compete in gymnastics.

GLOSSARY

ALL-AROUND
When gymnasts compete in all of the events as an individual. The all-around champion earns the most points from all the events combined.

DEDUCTION
When points are taken off a gymnast's score.

ELITE GYMNASTICS
The top level of gymnastics where gymnasts can compete internationally for their countries, such as in the Olympics.

FLOOR EXERCISE
An event in which gymnasts perform tumbling skills and dance elements on a spring-filled square mat.

ROTATION
In gymnastics competitions, squads move from event to event to compete. Each movement to a new event is called a rotation.

UNEVEN BARS
An event in which female gymnasts swing between two bars of unequal height.

VAULT
An event in which gymnasts push off a table and do flips and twists in the air.

MORE INFORMATION

BOOKS

Lawrence, Blythe. *Total Gymnastics*. Minneapolis, MN: Abdo Publishing, 2017.

Nicks, Erin. *A Guide to Competitive Gymnastics*. Minneapolis, MN: Abdo Publishing, 2020.

Schlegel, Elfi, and Claire Ross Dunn. *The Gymnastics Book: The Young Performer's Guide to Gymnastics*. New York: Firefly Books, 2018.

ONLINE RESOURCES

To learn more about women's college gymnastics, please visit abdobooklinks.com or scan this QR code. These links are routinely monitored and updated to provide the most current information available.

INDEX

All-American, 29
American Cup, 8
balance beam, 10, 14, 20, 27
elite gymnasts, 7, 9–10, 12, 21–23, 26–28
ESPYs, 6
floor exercise, 4, 6, 7, 9–10, 14, 20, 23, 26
gym slams, 26, 28
Kocian, Madison, 26–27
Kupets Carter, Courtney, 28–29
National Collegiate Athletic Association (NCAA), 12–14, 16–17, 18–21, 26, 27–29
National Collegiate Gymnastics Association, 17, 29
Nichols, Maggie, 27–28
Ohashi, Katelyn, 4, 6, 7–10
Olympic Games, 7, 9, 12, 18, 20, 23, 26–29
Ross, Kyla, 24–28
scoring, 7, 14–16, 18–23, 26–28
teams, 6–7, 10, 12, 14–15, 18, 20–22, 26–27, 29
uneven bars, 14, 27–28
University of California, Los Angeles (UCLA), 6–7, 9–10, 24–27
University of Georgia, 28–29
University of Oklahoma, 18, 27
vault, 14, 18, 26
World Championships, 27

ABOUT THE AUTHOR

Heather Rule is a writer, sports journalist, and social media coordinator. She has a bachelor's degree in journalism and mass communication from the University of St. Thomas.